D0512054

The Sleepover Club

Have you been invited to all these sleepovers?

Sleepover Club Down Under

by Narinder Dhami

Collins

An imprint of HarperCollins*Publishers*

The Sleepover Club ® is a
registered trademark of HarperCollins*Publishers* Ltd

First published in Great Britain by Collins in 2000
Collins is an imprint of HarperCollins*Publishers* Ltd
77-85 Fulham Palace Road, Hammersmith,
London, W6 8JB

The HarperCollins website address is
www.**fire**and**water**.com

3 5 7 9 8 6 4 2

Text copyright © Narinder Dhami 2000

Original series characters, plotlines
and settings © Rose Impey 1997

ISBN 0 00710628 9

The author asserts the moral right to
be identified as the author of the work.

Printed and bound in Great Britain by
Omnia Books Limited,
Glasgow

Conditions of Sale
This book is sold subject to the condition
that it shall not, by way of trade or otherwise,
be lent, re-sold, hired out or otherwise circulated
without the publisher's prior consent in any form,
binding or cover other than that in which it is
published and without a similar condition
including this condition being imposed
on the subsequent purchaser.

Sleepover Kit List

1. Sleeping bag
2. Pillow
3. Pyjamas or a nightdress
4. Slippers
5. Toothbrush, toothpaste, soap etc
6. Towel
7. Teddy
8. A creepy story
9. Food for a midnight feast:
   chocolate, crisps, sweets, biscuits.
   In fact anything you like to eat.
10. Torch
11. Hairbrush
12. Hair things like a bobble or hairband,
    if you need them
13. Clean knickers and socks
14. Change of clothes for the next day
15. Sleepover diary and membership card

CHAPTER ONE

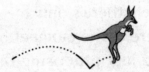

"Life is so hard
When you don't have that special someone
That's why I need you
To help me through…"

"Kenny, you're singing all the wrong words!" Fliss moaned.

"And why are you singing so much higher than the rest of us?" Lyndz wanted to know.

"Yeah, Kenny, you sound like a cat with a sore throat!" I added, sticking my fingers in my ears.

"Flippin' cheek!" Kenny grumbled. "I'll have you lot know I've got a fantastic voice –

7

my gran said I ought to be on the stage!"

"Yeah, sweeping it, maybe!" I joked, and ducked as Kenny flicked a choc chip cookie at me.

Hi there! So you found your way to Fliss's house OK, did you? Excellent! We were wondering where you'd got to. Come into the kitchen, and say hello to the rest of the Sleepover Club. Well, there's only me, Kenny, Fliss and Lyndz here at the moment because Rosie's late. We're just practising the song we want to sing in assembly at school next week – if we can shut Kenny up, that is! It's the theme tune from one of our fave programmes, that Australian soap opera *South Beach*. The words are a bit dodgy, but the tune's all right!

We're sleeping over at Fliss's tonight (we take it in turns to have a sleepover every week at one of our houses, that's why we're called the Sleepover Club – obviously). Anyway, you can see we were all pretty hyped up and being a bit loud and giggly. It was exciting stuff, what with Christmas coming up and our school panto (which you'll probably know about already!), but there was *another* reason why we were getting all over-excited. I'll give you a clue – roll those drums please, here it comes – *BRAD MARTIN*!

What do you mean, you don't know what I'm talking about? Oh, *please*! Where have you been all your life? You *have* to know who Brad Martin is! You watch *South Beach*, don't you? You don't? Oh. Well, I'll just have to explain *everything* then!

Anyway, like I said, there we all were round Fliss's, sitting in the kitchen drinking Sunny Delight and waiting for Rosie, and talking about what we wanted for Christmas.

"I really want a lizard!" Kenny said, and we all fell about laughing. We're used to Kenny being crazy, but sometimes she can still surprise us!

"What, a *real* one?" Fliss asked, wrinkling up her nose in disgust.

"No, a dead one!" Kenny retorted. "Of *course* I want a real one."

"Gross!" Fliss shuddered.

"That's what Molly the Monster says,"

9

Kenny replied with an evil grin. Molly's her sister, although Kenny wishes she wasn't. They're always trying to get one over on each other, and you know what Kenny's like – she usually wins!

"You only want a lizard to annoy Molly," Lyndz pointed out.

"So?" Kenny shrugged. "That's a good reason!"

"It's not very nice for the lizard!" I said. "And anyway, Kenny, your pets never survive!"

It's true. Kenny's got the killer touch where pets are concerned.

"My mum says I can have loads of new clothes," Fliss said, "and I want some boots and some make-up as well."

Kenny groaned. "You're so *girly*, Felicity!"

Kenny thinks that's the worst insult she can give anyone. If someone called *her* 'girly', she'd thump them, but Fliss actually looked quite pleased!

"So?" she said. " I *am* a girl!"

Just then Fliss's mum waddled in from the living room. It wasn't long before the babies were born, and Mrs Proudlove's tummy was so big, I was surprised she could walk!

"More biscuits, girls?" she enquired. "Or would you like some doughnuts?"

"Both, please!" Kenny said.

"I bet you can't wait for the twins to be born, Fliss," Lyndz remarked.

"Yeah," Kenny said wickedly. "*Two* lots of smelly nappies to change!"

Fliss looked sick. I reckoned she'd faint away dead on the spot if she had to change a dirty nappy! Mind you, she *did* change Rosie's neighbour's baby's nappy once, but that was ages ago.

"Where's Rosie got to?" I wondered. "If she doesn't hurry up, she's going to miss…"

"*SOUTH BEACH!*" the others yelled, and we all rushed into the living room to grab the best seat on the sofa.

I can't believe you've never seen *South Beach*. It was one of our best programmes – we liked it just as much as *Neighbours* and *Home and Away*. Anyway, Kenny got the best seat by elbowing everyone else out of the way.

"Ow!" Fliss said crossly, hopping round the

living room holding her foot. "Kenny, you trod on my toe, you idiot!"

"And you elbowed me in the ribs!" I grumbled, plonking myself down next to Kenny and elbowing her back.

"Ssh, it's starting!" Lyndz said, calming everyone down as usual.

"Life is so hard
When you don't have that special someone
That's why I need you
To help me through…"

We all started singing the theme tune (well, yelling it really) and Mrs Proudlove waddled as fast as she could into the kitchen and shut the door. What a cheek – I didn't think our singing was *that* bad.

I suppose *South Beach* wasn't really that different to *Neighbours* or *Home and Away*. It was set in a beach café, and it had loads of good-looking people in it who all had big problems with their families and friends, just like the other two programmes. But *South Beach* did have ONE thing that *Neighbours* and *Home and Away* didn't – and that was Brad Martin, the hunkiest guy in the entire universe!

"Ooh, Brad Martin's so gorgeous!" Fliss drooled as the credits started and fit-looking surfers ran along the beach with their boards. At the front was Brad Martin, who played Rick, a waiter at the beach café. He's got long blond hair and blue eyes and Fliss loves him even more than Ryan Scott, who's in our class at school. Even Kenny thinks he's gorgeous, although she won't admit it.

"He's cute!" I agreed.

"He's OK – for a guy!" Kenny snorted, pretending not to be interested.

"I wonder if he'll be just as gorgeous in real life?" Lyndz said hopefully.

Remember I told you that there was something else we were really excited about, apart from our sleepover that night? Well, we were actually going to see Brad in the flesh! No, *really*! I nearly *died* when I read in the local newspaper a few months ago that he was coming to Leicester to appear in the panto *Aladdin*. Leicester's the nearest big city to Cuddington, the village where we all live, so I pestered my mum and dad for ages to take us *all* to see him. They finally agreed, although I had to promise to do the vacuuming for a week. We were going to the panto near the end of the Christmas holidays before we went back to school, and we could hardly wait.

"So who do you think Rick's going to choose?" Fliss asked as the programme started.

At the moment Rick was in love with two different girls, and we were dying to know which one he was going to go out with.

"Charlene," said Kenny immediately.

"No, Melanie," Fliss argued.

"Melanie's too girly," Kenny retorted. That was just why Fliss liked her!

"Well, Charlene's too much of a tomboy," Fliss pointed out. "And anyway, she's still in love with Tony."

"I thought Charlene didn't like Tony any more after she found out he swindled Mr and Mrs Williams out of all that money," I objected.

"That wasn't Tony's fault," Lyndz reminded me, "Luke set him up."

"I thought Luke fancied Melanie anyway," Kenny put in.

"No, Luke fancies Noelene," I interrupted her, "only he doesn't know that Noelene's secretly married to Andrew."

"Ssh, we're missing it!" Fliss wailed as Rick began to have a row with Melanie about Charlene.

The rest of the programme wasn't that good (because those were the bits Brad Martin wasn't in), but Luke asked Noelene out and Andrew hit him, which was quite exciting. Then at the end of the programme, Rick had a row with Charlene about Melanie, and he went out on his surfboard on his own. He fell off and hit his head and the programme finished with him lying unconscious on the beach.

"Oh no!" Fliss gasped, looking worried. "I hope he's OK."

"Yeah, bound to be," Kenny said. "He looked OK when I saw him in the newspaper last week, opening that new supermarket in Leicester!"

Fliss gave her a shove. "I mean, I hope they don't kill him off in the programme!"

"There'd be a riot if they did!" Lyndz said.

"I wish I could've gone to see Brad opening

that supermarket," I grumbled. "But my mum wouldn't let me have the day off school. Typical!"

My mum and dad are both lawyers, which is a real pain. Have you ever tried winning an argument against *two* lawyers?

"Brad must be staying in Leicester while he's doing the panto," Lyndz said hopefully. "Maybe we'll see him while we're out shopping with our parents or something."

That's Lyndz all over – she always looks on the bright side!

"Some chance!" Kenny scoffed. "Leicester's *huge*! Tell you what though…" she grinned at us. "Maybe we'll be able to go backstage and get his autograph after we've been to the panto!"

We all got pretty excited then!

"Do you think we'll be allowed?" Fliss gasped.

Kenny shrugged. "Maybe, maybe not. But I'll think of a wicked plan to get us in, don't worry!"

Fliss, Lyndz and I were worrying already. Kenny's plans aren't exactly foolproof – or even legal, half the time.

"Where on earth has Rosie got to?" Lyndz asked.

"Maybe I'd better give her a call," Fliss suggested, but right then the doorbell rang.

"About time too!" Kenny moaned as Fliss went to answer it. "We can't have a proper sleepover with one person missing!"

Next moment we heard Rosie apologising breathlessly in the hall.

"Sorry, Fliss! Mum's car broke down, and we had to wait for the AA to come and you'll never guess what happened— OW!"

There was a loud crash, and Lyndz, Kenny and me rushed out into the hall to see what was going on. Rosie was sprawled on the hall carpet, while Fliss was in stitches.

"She tripped over the rug!" Fliss spluttered helplessly.

"Felicity!" Mrs Proudlove hurried out of the kitchen. "Don't just stand there laughing, help Rosie up!"

Fliss hauled Rosie to her feet, while the rest of us stood around trying not to snigger.

"You'll never *guess* what happened—" Rosie began again.

"So tell us!" I said as we went into the living room. To be honest, I wasn't expecting anything that exciting. Rosie gets wound up over nothing at all sometimes. "You look like you're about to burst!"

"Yeah, you're as red as a ripe tomato!" Kenny told her helpfully, but Rosie wasn't listening. She looked round at us all, her eyes wide.

"I saw *Brad Martin*!" she announced. "Right here in Cuddington!"

CHAPTER TWO

No-one said anything at first, not even Kenny. But I guessed that the others were thinking exactly the same thing as me – that Rosie had gone completely nuts!

Meanwhile Rosie was frowning at us.

"Didn't you hear me?" she began. "I said—"

"Oh, we heard what you said all right," Kenny interrupted her. "We just don't believe it, that's all!"

"Yeah, nice try, Rosie," I added. "You really had us going there – for about two seconds!"

Rosie turned red. "I'm not winding you up," she snapped. "I really *did* see Brad Martin!"

"So what did you do? Ask him where his surfboard was?" Fliss asked sarcastically.

"Oh, give up, Rosie!" Kenny snorted. "Nobody believes you!"

"You must've made a mistake," Lyndz said kindly.

Rosie looked absolutely furious, and that was what made me stop and think. I mean, Rosie likes the odd wind-up, but she'd never tried to pull anything like this before.

"OK, Rosie, tell us *exactly* what happened," I said, glaring at Kenny and the others to make sure they got the message. Kenny rolled her eyes as if to say *You're as barmy as she is!* But she didn't say anything out loud.

"Well, Mum's car broke down in Riverside Avenue," Rosie explained, "and she went to the phonebox to call the AA. I was sitting in the car, and I saw Brad go past—"

Kenny couldn't keep quiet any longer. "Oh, pull the other one – it's got ten million bells on it!" she exclaimed.

"Are you sure it was Brad, Rosie?" I asked. "It could have been someone who looked like him."

"No, it was him," Rosie replied immediately, "I know it was!"

She sounded pretty convincing. I looked at Fliss and Lyndz. They were both looking doubtful, as if they didn't know what to believe. Meanwhile, Kenny was still certain that it was a wind-up.

"OK, so what was he wearing?" she asked.

"Jeans, a black fleece and a black baseball cap," Rosie snapped.

Kenny pounced straight away. "If he was wearing a baseball cap, how do you know it was Brad?" she pointed out triumphantly.

"I got a good look at his face as he walked towards the car," Rosie retorted.

We all looked at each other. Rosie was obviously convinced that she *had* seen Brad Martin.

"Why didn't you get out and run after him?" Kenny asked suspiciously.

"Because my mum was coming back by then, and she stopped me," Rosie said sulkily.

"Oh!" Fliss squealed all of a sudden.

"What is it?" we all chorused.

"Well, what if—?" Fliss stopped. "No, he *couldn't* be!"

"Couldn't what?" we all repeated impatiently.

"Well…" Fliss hopped from one foot to the other. "I suppose he *might* be…"

"MIGHT BE WHAT?" the rest of us repeated. I was beginning to feel like Polly the Parrot!

"Well, we were saying before that Brad must be staying nearby if he's in the panto," Fliss finally managed to get the words out. "Maybe he's staying in Cuddington!"

Rosie nearly fainted away on the spot. "He *can't* be! Can he?"

"Yes! That must be it!" Lyndz agreed, looking excited.

"But if he *is* in Cuddington, where would he be staying?" I asked doubtfully.

Before anyone could reply, Fliss's mum came in with a cup of tea and a magazine.

"Still here, girls?" she asked brightly. "I thought you were going upstairs to Fliss's room."

"We are." I jumped to my feet, dragging Kenny with me. "Come on, you lot."

We all legged it upstairs and into Fliss's bedroom. Once we were inside, Fliss closed the door and we all piled on to the bed and started whispering to each other. We were getting really excited by this time, although Kenny still wasn't totally convinced.

"Do you really think Brad's in Cuddington?" Lyndz asked.

"I *know* he is!" Rosie replied.

"Maybe we should go and look for him," I suggested.

"I'll *die* if I see him!" Fliss added.

"Why are we whispering?" Kenny wanted to know.

"In case anyone else finds out!" I told her. "This is one big secret!"

Kenny frowned. "Hey, hang on a minute," she said. "If Rosie's seen Brad in Cuddington, how come no-one else has?"

"What do you mean?" Fliss asked.

"Well, other people must have seen him too," Kenny pointed out, "and no-one at school's mentioned it. It'd be all over the place in five minutes flat if they had!"

"The panto only started a week or two

ago," Fliss pointed out. "He might only just have moved in."

"Yeah, we'll get the latest when we go back to school on Monday," I said. "Someone else *might* have seen him – we just haven't heard about it yet."

"Well, if Brad *is* here, where would he be staying?" Kenny wasn't giving in that easily. "There aren't any really posh hotels in Cuddington."

That threw us a bit.

"He might be staying at Buckingham House," Rosie suggested.

Kenny burst out laughing. "What, with Mrs Windsor? He'd have to be desperate!"

Buckingham House is a B&B in Cuddington, and it's probably the poshest guest house in the village. But the lady who runs it, Mrs Windsor, is a right old snob – I reckon she called it Buckingham House because she thinks she's the queen of Cuddington!

"I've got it!" Fliss suddenly bounced off the bed. "Why don't we ring the theatre? They'll be able to tell us where Brad's staying!"

"Good idea." Kenny jumped up too. "Give me the phone!"

Fliss has just got her own girly pink phone in her bedroom and she's dead proud of it. Anyway, Kenny grabbed the receiver, and Fliss went to get the phone book, but she started moaning when she came back.

"It's my phone, Kenny. I ought to make the call!"

Kenny raised her eyebrows at her. "Can you do a posh grown-up voice?"

"No," Fliss muttered.

"OK, here goes." Kenny tapped in the number of the theatre, and we all waited, holding our breath until we heard the phone being picked up at the other end. Kenny immediately pinched her nose with her fingers, and said, "Hello? Who is this please?" in this really posh voice.

"It's the doorman at the theatre!" she hissed at us, covering the mouthpiece. Then she pinched her nose again and said grandly, "This is Brad Martin's aunt speaking. I need to get in touch with him, so kindly tell me where he lives!"

Meanwhile the rest of us were rolling around on Fliss's bed, stuffing our hands in our mouths to stop ourselves from laughing.

"I see," Kenny said after a moment or two. "Well, thank you very much." And she put the phone down.

"Did he give you the address?" I asked eagerly.

"Is Brad staying in Cuddington?" Rosie chimed in.

"Or is he in Leicester?" Lyndz asked.

"Don't keep us in suspense, Kenny!" Fliss begged.

"The doorman said I was about the tenth person to ring today trying to find out where Brad was staying, and to stop pestering him!" Kenny said.

Our faces fell.

"So how can we find out?" Rosie asked.

"Well, we can't do anything now," I pointed out. "Anyway, aren't we supposed to be having a sleepover?"

But it turned out that the sleepover was pretty much a wash-out after that, because all we did was talk about whether or not

Brad could *really* be staying in Cuddington. We had a sort of half-hearted pillow fight and we had a midnight feast and we wrote in our diaries and we did all the kinds of things we normally do, but we weren't really interested. There was only one thing we wanted to know. Where was Brad Martin? By this time, i think we were all convinced that Rosie *had* seen him – even Kenny!

It was only when we were in our sleeping bags on Fliss's floor that I started to have second thoughts. We'd just sung our sleepover song, and everyone was getting a bit drowsy.

"Maybe I didn't see Brad after all," Rosie said suddenly in a low voice. "Maybe it *was* someone else…"

But I don't think anyone heard her except me.

Wait until you hear what happened when we got to school on Monday morning. It was really weird!

We all met up in the playground as usual, and we were *still* going on about Brad Martin, and where he might be staying in Cuddington. We'd spent most of Sunday on the phone to each other too, discussing the very same thing, until our parents put their feet down. My dad had said that he'd gag me if I didn't shut up about it!

"I reckon we should go over to Buckingham House after school and check it out," Kenny suggested as we all sat down on the playground wall. "We might see Brad leaving for the theatre."

"Don't let Mrs Windsor catch us though," Fliss said, looking alarmed.

"Why?" Kenny said with a grin. "Are you scared of her, Flissy?"

Fliss blushed. "A bit," she muttered

"Well, she can't stop us hanging around outside her house," I said firmly. "It's a public footpath!"

"Yeah, and if Brad's there, we'll soon find out!" Kenny added, and we all cheered. Except Rosie.

"Um – maybe it wasn't Brad," Rosie muttered, looking embarrassed. "Maybe I got it wrong after all…"

"Well, there's no harm in trying to find out, is there?" I said quickly, not wanting Rosie to feel bad about it.

"I've brought my autograph book," Lyndz added. "It'll be nice to get a proper autograph in it, I've only got you lot so far!"

"Flippin' cheek!" Kenny snorted. Then she winked at us. "Sssh! Don't say anything about Brad in front of the Gruesome Twosome!"

The M&Ms, Emma Hughes and Emily Berryman, were walking across the playground in our general direction. They're in our class, but that's about all we've got in common with them – *we're* not snooty, stuck-up snobs! Nobody likes them except Alana 'Banana' Palmer, and that's because she's just about the doziest person in Cuddington Primary. But the weird thing was that today, the M&Ms were being followed across the playground by a huge crowd of kids, tagging along behind them as if they were the bee's knees.

I frowned. "Why are all those kids following the Queen and the Goblin?"

29

"Maybe Emma's been nice to someone at last," Kenny suggested. "That'd draw a crowd!"

The M&Ms were looking well smug. They saw us sitting on the wall and grinned at each other in that incredibly sly way they have.

"We know something you don't know!" Emily Berryman (the Goblin) chanted in her gruff voice.

"I know lots of things *you* don't know, Emily," Kenny retorted. "That's because you're really, really thick!"

We started giggling, and so did the whole crowd of kids. The Goblin turned purple and the Queen stuck her nose in the air like she always does.

"Oh, you think you're so clever, Kenny!" Emma Hughes sniffed. "Well, we *do* know something you don't know and we're not going to tell you, so there!"

"Hey, Kenny," said Alana Banana, strolling up next to the Queen. "Did you know that Emily saw that surfer guy from *South Beach* in Cuddington yesterday?"

I glanced at the others. So the Goblin had seen him too! That was why all those kids were following her. It was true – Brad *was* in Cuddington!

"You mean Brad Martin," I said as coolly as I could.

"Yeah, that's him," Alana agreed.

The Goblin was now the colour of an aubergine. "What did you tell *them* for, Alana?" she howled.

"Everyone else knows." Alana Banana pointed at the crowd of kids behind them. "You said you wanted to tell *everyone*."

"Yes, but not *them*!" Emma Hughes snapped, looking as if she was about to rip Alana Banana's head off.

"Bet you didn't really see him anyway!" called someone in the crowd.

"Yeah, it's a wind-up, isn't it, Emily?" added Ryan Scott. He was with his mate Danny McCloud, who's also in our class.

"Well, I saw him too—" Rosie began. "OW!"

I didn't see what happened, but I guessed Kenny had elbowed her to shut her up. After all, why should we help the Gruesome Twosome out?

"I *did* see him!" the Goblin snapped.

"Well, did you get his autograph?" Danny demanded.

"No, I couldn't," Emily muttered. "I was in the car with my dad, and he wouldn't stop. But it was definitely Brad Martin, and he was wearing a black fleece, jeans and a black baseball cap!"

"Never mind, Em." The Queen linked arms with the Goblin, and threw us another haughty stare. "We'll soon find out where he's staying, and when we've got his autograph, everyone will *have* to believe you!"

Then the M&Ms swanned off again. The crowd of kids still scurried after them though, trying to find out if it was a wind-up or not.

"Did you hear that?" Fliss gasped. "Emily described Brad wearing exactly the same clothes as Rosie did! It *must* have been him!"

"I knew it was!" Rosie said triumphantly.

Kenny was frowning. "Yeah, but the question is – how are we going to find out where Brad's staying before the M&Ms do?"

CHAPTER THREE

Well, now that we were pretty sure Brad Martin was somewhere in Cuddington, there was no stopping us! And we were determined to see him before the M&Ms did, and get his autograph. The trouble was, half the kids in the school had the same idea, by the sound of it. Everyone was planning search parties around Cuddington to see if they could flush Brad out of his hiding place. Then a rumour started that a couple of kids in Year Four had seen him in the village on Sunday evening near to the B&B, Buckingham House, and that set everyone off again.

"There's going to be a whole crowd of kids charging off to Buckingham House after school today," Kenny grumbled as we walked back to class after assembly. "We haven't got a chance of finding Brad first!"

"What's all this fuss about Brad Martin anyway?" Ryan Scott grumbled. We all looked round, and he winked at Fliss, who giggled. "I'm better-looking than he is any day!"

"No, you're not, Ryan," I said. "No-one wants *your* autograph!"

"Fliss does!" Kenny chimed in.

"Shut up, Kenny!" Fliss hissed, and gave her a shove which sent her smack into Emily Berryman.

"You did that on purpose, Laura McKenzie!" the Goblin growled.

"Yes, you're just jealous because Emily saw Brad Martin and you didn't," the Queen added, stirring as usual.

Kenny didn't get a chance to say anything because our teacher, Mrs Weaver, was glaring at us as we went into class. She wasn't too happy because we were all mega-excited and wouldn't shut up. She probably thought we were all hyped up about Christmas coming. Little did she know!

"QUIET!" Mrs Weaver yelled, getting fed up as we took ages to settle down. "I don't know what's the matter with you all today."

"I wonder if Mrs Weaver fancies Brad?" Kenny whispered, and that set us Sleepovers off *again*. It was only when Mrs W gave us one of her drop-dead stares that we shut up.

"Right, we've got a lot to do today," Mrs Weaver said briskly. "We're delivering our Christmas parcels to pensioners this morning."

In all the excitement about Brad, I'd forgotten about the Christmas parcels. As well as our Food for the Homeless project, we'd been collecting tins and packets of food for elderly people in the village, and today we were going round to give them out, so that meant a whole morning off school. Excellent!

Mrs Weaver went round the classroom dividing people up into groups and handing out the parcels. Meanwhile, we carried on discussing the only thing we could talk about at the moment – Brad!

"Do you really think he's staying at Buckingham House?" Lyndz asked.

Kenny frowned. "I dunno. I mean, who'd put up with snobby old Mrs Windsor for five minutes? *Especially* an Australian mega-star!"

"Those kids in Year Four said they saw him by the B&B, though," I reminded her.

"Or maybe he's staying with someone in the village," Rosie suggested.

We carried on talking about Brad as we lined up to leave the classroom. I was carrying our parcel, and it weighed a flippin' ton!

"I wonder if we'll see Brad *now*?" Fliss said eagerly as Mrs Weaver led us out of the playground and into the street. It looked like everyone in the class had the same idea, because they were all looking round eagerly as Mrs W led us along the road.

"Watch this!" Kenny whispered. Then, raising her voice, she gasped, "Look! Who's that over there?"

"Where? Where?" squealed Emma Hughes,

whose ears were flapping like Dumbo the elephant's. Emily Berryman spun round to see what was going on, and whacked the Queen hard with the box she was carrying. Meanwhile, Alana Banana stopped dead and looked round too, and Mrs Weaver bumped straight into her.

"Really, girls!" Mrs Weaver snapped, glaring at all three of them. "Could you please look where you're going!"

"Result!" Kenny whispered, grinning all over her face.

Anyway, we didn't see Brad, as you've probably guessed. Mrs Weaver started sending groups of kids into different houses, and telling them to hand over the parcel and wait there till she came back to collect them. We were the very last group to be dropped off, at a little house right on the edge of the village.

"This parcel's for Mrs Andrews," Mrs Weaver told us, looking at her list. "Wait here, and I'll be back to collect you in about twenty minutes."

"Hey, you lot!" Kenny whispered excitedly

as Rosie rang the doorbell. "You know where we are, don't you?"

"Yes, outside Mrs Andrews' house," I replied.

"All right, smartypants, I didn't mean that." Kenny pointed down the street. "Buckingham House is just round the corner."

We all gasped. Kenny was right. We were only a few minutes' walk away from where Brad Martin just *might* be staying!

"Maybe we'll get a chance to nip round there before Weaver comes back!" Kenny whispered, just as the front door opened.

"Oh, hello, girls, are you from Cuddington Primary?" A little old lady with white hair and twinkling blue eyes stood there, smiling at us.

"Yes, we've brought you a Christmas parcel," I said, holding it out.

"Oh, how kind." Mrs Andrews opened the door wider. "Do come in."

We all trooped into the little house. As we went in, Kenny whispered, "We'll leg it before Weaver gets back and go round to Buck House!" and we all nodded.

"Well, let's see what you've brought me," Mrs Andrews beamed, opening up the box. I was glad to put it down at last – my arms were about to drop off!

"Biscuits, cakes, tins of veg…" Mrs Andrews began unpacking the stuff. "But where's my bottle of gin?"

We all stared at her with our mouths open, even Kenny!

"Just joking, girls!" Mrs Andrews winked at us, and we all grinned.

"So come and sit down and tell me all about yourselves," she went on, so we all piled on to the big sofa. It was only a little living room, but it was stuffed with furniture, and there were loads of those old black and white photos on the wall.

"When's your teacher coming back for you?" Mrs Andrews asked.

"In ten minutes' time," Kenny said, glancing at the rest of us. That gave us about ten minutes to get round to Buckingham House and check it out.

"What's she like, your teacher?" Mrs Andrews opened a packet of shortbread and handed it round. "Is she a bit of a dragon?"

"A bit!" said Rosie. "But she's OK."

"I remember the teacher I had when I was your age," Mrs Andrews said. "Mr Church, his name was. Used to rap our knuckles with his cane if we weren't listening!"

"He didn't!" Fliss gasped, her eyes as big as saucers.

"He did," Mrs Andrews said with a smile. "But we got our own back on him – we used to play tricks on him all the time!"

"What kind of tricks?" Kenny asked eagerly. You know how much she loves playing tricks herself!

"Well, once we changed the blackboard chalk for joke chalk," Mrs Andrews replied. "It just wouldn't write, and Mr Church went mad! He made us all stay in and do lines. Then another time we polished the floor round his desk so it was all slippery, and he kept sliding about all over the place!"

"Cool!" Kenny grinned.

Mrs Andrews had loads of other stories to tell us about her horrible teacher, and we were so interested, we nearly forgot all about going to Buck House! But then Kenny nudged me and nodded at the clock.

"We've got to go, Mrs Andrews." I jumped to my feet. "But we'll come back and visit you in the Christmas holidays, if that's all right?"

I glanced at the others, and they nodded.

"I'll look forward to it," Mrs Andrews said. "And don't let your teacher catch you doing whatever it is you're going off to do, will you?"

We all stopped dead, just as we were about to go out of the front door. I bumped into Fliss, Fliss bumped into Rosie, Rosie bumped into Lyndz and Kenny, who was right at the back, bumped into all four of us.

"What do you mean?" I spluttered.

Mrs Andrews grinned at us. "I might be old, but I can still hear all right! Off you go, and remember to come back and see me soon."

"She's so cool, isn't she?" Fliss said as we dashed down the path. "For an old lady, I mean."

"Yeah, she must have overheard what you

said to me when we went in, Kenny," I remembered.

"Maybe we can run some errands for her or something, when we visit her again," Lyndz chimed in.

"Yeah, she looks like she's on her own a lot, doesn't she?" Kenny added. "Come on, we'll have to get a move on or Weaver'll catch us!"

"I hope we find Brad," Fliss said as we hurried round the corner. "Then we can really rub the M&Ms' snobby noses in it!"

"Pity we didn't bring a camera," Kenny grumbled. "A photo of the Sleepover Club with Brad Martin would have been excellent!"

Buckingham House was a massive, old-fashioned place with a big garden. We opened the posh iron gate and hurried up the drive. But before we'd got halfway up the path, the front door flew open.

"Oh no, it's Mrs Windsor!" Fliss moaned, looking scared to death.

"What do you want?" The landlady stood in the doorway, glaring at us. She was only about five feet tall, but I knew what Fliss meant. She *was* scary!

Kenny was the bravest. "Hello, Mrs Windsor," she said politely, "We're looking for—"

"I know who you're looking for!" Mrs Windsor snapped, her face red. "That Australian actor who's in the pantomime!"

"Oh, is he staying here?" I asked eagerly, and Mrs Windsor turned from red to purple.

"No, he isn't!" she shouted. "I've had kids coming round knocking on my door all morning and I'm fed up with it!" She advanced down the path towards us, and we all took a step backwards. "You can tell all your friends that Brad whatever-his-name-is isn't staying here, has never stayed here and never WILL stay here!"

And she stormed into the house and banged the door shut.

"Looks like Brad's not staying there, then!" Kenny said gloomily as we walked back to Mrs Andrews' house.

"Maybe he's just not staying in Cuddington at all," Fliss said sadly.

"Oh-oh, trouble!" I whispered, as we turned the corner.

Mrs Weaver was standing by Mrs Andrews' gate, glaring at us.

"Where have you been, girls?" she enquired in a freezing tone. "You were told to wait here till I came back for you."

"Mrs Andrews felt a bit tired, so we left her alone and went for a walk," I said. It was a bit feeble, but it was the best I could do.

"Next time do as you're told," Mrs W snapped. "Now hurry up, the others are waiting for us at the end of the street."

"I've had enough of Brad Martin," Rosie muttered as we followed Mrs Weaver down the road. "All he's done so far is get us into trouble!"

"At least we'll get to see him in *Aladdin*," Fliss pointed out.

"Let's forget all about finding him, and concentrate on Christmas and the school panto," I suggested.

"Good idea," Lyndz agreed.

"Yeah, Brad *can't* be in Cuddington,"

Kenny added. "It must be someone who just looks like him."

We all agreed with that.

But as it turned out, things weren't quite that simple...

CHAPTER FOUR

So what did you get for Christmas? I did OK! I got loads of clothes, a new CD player and a pair of cool purple and silver trainers I'd wanted for *ages*. I also got a purple hand-knitted jumper from my gran which was about ten sizes too big! But my best present was a fake dog mess from Kenny. I put it right under the tree on Christmas morning, and my dad nearly had a fit when he saw it. He blamed our spaniel Pepsi, and went to get some kitchen roll to clean it up. I nearly *died* laughing.

What do you mean, what about Brad Martin? Oh, well, we were still really looking forward to seeing him in the panto before we went back to school, but we'd been so busy getting ready for Christmas and our school panto that we hadn't really had time to think about much else. Sure, someone would come to school every so often and say they'd seen Brad in Cuddington, but we knew it was all a wind-up. No-one had managed to get an autograph or a photo of him, although Danny McCloud went round on the last day of term waving a piece of paper in the air, saying he'd seen Brad and got his autograph. Only Alana Banana was daft enough to believe him – the rest of us didn't think Brad would have signed his name as *Bard Martin*. Danny's rubbish at spelling.

We'd had our last sleepover before Christmas, and we didn't know when we were going to get another one. You know what Christmas is like – you have to go and visit all your relations, and they all come and stay with you, so none of our parents were up for a sleepover. When I asked my mum, she said she wanted a nice, quiet Christmas with no hassle, and that meant no

47

sleepovers – what a cheek! Especially since we had Gran staying with us, and she'd drunk a bit too much sherry and knocked the Christmas tree over. Even Kenny doesn't cause that much trouble. But anyway, even though we couldn't have a sleepover, we all arranged to meet up the day after Boxing Day, round at my place…

"Thanks for the dog mess, Kenny," I said as we all piled on to the sofa in the living room. Well, me, Kenny, Fliss and Lyndz did. Rosie was late again. "It was my best prezzie – it really fooled my dad!"

"I put mine under the kitchen table when my mum was cooking the Christmas dinner," Lyndz chimed in. "She thought Buster had done it!"

"Did you give *everyone* fake dog messes for Chrissie?" I asked Kenny.

"Nah – only people who've got dogs," Kenny replied. "I'm not *that* stupid!"

"So what did *you* get from Kenny, Fliss?" Lyndz asked. Fliss hasn't got any animals at all – unless you count her boring goldfish and her pesky little brother, Callum.

"*The Floating Fly*," Fliss replied.

"It's a plastic fly," Kenny explained. "You drop it in someone's drink."

"Oh, you must have really *loved* that, Fliss!" I grinned.

"I did actually," Fliss agreed. "I put it in Callum's Coke, and when he saw it, he freaked! He dropped the glass, and the Coke went all over my cousin Carl!"

"Nice one, Flissy," Kenny beamed. I think she was really pleased her prezzies had been put to such good use!

"Your new trainers are cool, Frankie," Lyndz said, looking down at my feet.

"Yeah, class," Kenny agreed. "I got a Leicester City scarf and sports bag, some computer games and a new bike."

"I got a new riding hat and some jodhpurs," Lyndz chimed in. "And Mum and Dad bought a computer for me and my brothers."

Fliss took a deep breath. "I got two pairs of shoes, a pair of boots, a pink jumper, this skirt I'm wearing, a new handbag, three cuddly toys, a silver bracelet, a—"

"Quick, shut her up!" Kenny groaned,

grabbing a cushion and smothering Fliss with it. "Or we'll be here all day!"

I glanced at the clock. "Where's Rosie got to this time?" I wondered. "She knows we're going to visit Mrs Andrews this afternoon."

We'd fixed it all up with our parents, who seemed quite keen. I think they were glad to get rid of us. Dr McKenzie, Kenny's dad, knew Mrs Andrews because she was one of his patients, and he'd told us that most of the old lady's family lived abroad, so she was on her own a lot.

Kenny snorted. "She's probably going to come dashing in and tell us she saw Father Christmas in Cuddington!"

We couldn't help laughing.

"I wonder where Brad Martin *is* staying—" Fliss began, and this time we *all* grabbed a cushion and started whacking her.

"Stop it!" Fliss squealed. "I didn't say he was in Cuddington – I just wondered where he was staying, that's all!"

"It's a real pain *South Beach* isn't on at the moment," I grumbled. Although it was usually on daily, the soap had been taken off for a week or two over Christmas – right at a really exciting bit too. Brad was still in hospital after his accident, and an escaped convict had broken into Andrew and Noelene's house, and was holding them hostage.

"I hope Brad – I mean Rick – is OK," Fliss said anxiously. "The doctor wasn't sure if he'd ever surf again!"

"Hey, I've had a great idea," Kenny said suddenly. "Why don't we have an Australian sleepover? In honour of Brad Martin!"

Every so often Kenny comes up with a really *fab* idea! And that makes up for all the times her ideas have got us into big trouble!

"That'd be cool!" Fliss said eagerly "We could dress up in our summer clothes, and pretend it's hot."

"We could watch *South Beach* and *Neighbours*," I added eagerly, "and we could get some other videos like *Strictly Ballroom* and *Crocodile Dundee*. They're Australian films."

"We could have a barbie in the garden!" Lyndz chimed in.

"What, in this weather?" said Fliss in surprise.

"Why not? Your mum did it for us in January once, remember?" I said.

"I'll make myself a hat with corks hanging off it," Kenny decided. "And I'll bring some wichity grubs for the midnight feast!"

"Wichity grubs?" Fliss asked. "What are those?"

"They're these little white maggoty-looking insects that Aborigines eat," Kenny said airily. "They're supposed to taste really nice."

Fliss turned green. "Don't be gross, Kenny!"

"So where are we going to have this Australian sleepover, then?" Lyndz asked. "We can't have it at mine – we've got my grandparents over from Holland."

"And we've got Auntie Paula, Carl and Colin at ours," Fliss said.

"My gran and grandad are staying too," Kenny added.

"Don't look at me," I shrugged. "We've got my gran here as well."

Right on cue Gran walked in, carrying a cup of tea and a plate of Hob-Nobs. "Oh, hello, girls. Do you mind if I put the telly on? I don't want to miss *Supermarket Sweep*."

"We'll leave you to it, Gran," I said hastily. "Come on, let's go up to my room." But as we made for the stairs, the doorbell rang, and kept on ringing like someone had their finger glued to it.

"That'll be Rosie," Kenny predicted confidently.

"What's up with *her*?" I covered my ears as I rushed to open the door. If she woke Izzy up, my mum would go bananas.

"Maybe she *did* see Father Christmas after all!" Kenny grinned.

I opened the door, and Rosie dashed in.

"You'll nebber believe what I've god to dell you!" she gabbled. Her face was bright red, especially her nose – she was either really excited or she had a very bad cold!

"Speak English, can't you, Rudolph!" Kenny said, and we all grinned.

"Sorry, I've god a really, really bad code!" Rosie pulled out a pretty revolting-looking hanky and blew her nose. Don't worry, I'll translate for you from now on! "I think I know where Brad Martin's staying in Cuddington!"

We all groaned.

"Oh, don't start *that* again," Kenny muttered.

"No, it's true!" Rosie assured us. "It's really obvious – I don't know why I didn't think of it before!"

"Where then?" I asked curiously.

"The Haunted House!" Rosie replied.

None of us were expecting *that*. The Haunted House is what we call this massive old Victorian house near Rosie's place. It's got a long, winding driveway and huge gardens which are all overgrown. No-one's lived there for ages – it's been boarded up for years, and I think even Kenny finds it a bit spooky. We always dare each other to go in when we go past, but not even Kenny's had the nerve to try it yet! And anyway, the gates are always locked.

"The Haunted House?" Lyndz repeated. "But that's a right dump!"

"Yeah, Brad wouldn't be seen dead in that dirty old ruin!" Fliss sniffed.

"Well, *someone's* living there now," Rosie said impatiently. "They've started tidying up the gardens and repainting the house. My mum says she thinks they've been there for a month or two, but no-one's really seen much of the new owner yet."

I looked at the others. Even though we'd decided that Brad couldn't *possibly* be in Cuddington, this definitely sounded promising!

"*And* I've seen this really posh car driving through the gates," Rosie went on. "It's got blacked-out windows so you can't see who's in there!"

"I guess Brad could be renting the Haunted House while he's in the panto," I said slowly.

"Or maybe he's bought it!" Lyndz said eagerly. "Lots of Aussie soap stars come to live in Britain!"

"So Brad *is* in Cuddington!" Fliss squealed, jumping up and down like a mad thing.

We all started cheering and doing high fives and slapping each other on the back until Gran came out of the living room and complained.

"I can't hear *Supermarket Sweep* with all this racket going on," she grumbled.

"Is that a bad thing?" Kenny asked innocently, and the rest of us giggled.

"So what do we do now?" Lyndz asked. "About Brad, I mean."

"Only one thing *to* do!" Kenny said confidently. "We go round and check out the Haunted House right now, before we go to visit Mrs Andrews…"

"I don't think this is such a good idea, Kenny," Fliss muttered, as we walked up to the big iron gates at the top of the Haunted House's driveway.

"Why not?" Kenny asked.

"Well…" Fliss looked worried. You know what she's like about ghosties and ghoulies. Even though she was dying to find Brad, I don't think she was too happy about him living in the Haunted House.

Kenny grinned. "Don't worry, Fliss. Brad'll save you if there's any ghosts around!"

We all peered down the winding driveway. It was lined with trees which were so big they met overhead and blocked out the sky, so it looked pretty spooky. We could just about see the house at the bottom of the drive, but there was no sign of anyone around.

"Look, we won't be able to get in," I said, pointing at the gates. There was a big sign on them which read *These gates are alarmed.*

"They don't look that worried to me – ha ha!" Kenny joked, and we all groaned.

"What shall we do, then?" Rosie asked.

"Hadn't we better go and see Mrs Andrews soon?" Lyndz put in anxiously.

"She said she'd be in all afternoon," I replied. "We've got loads of time."

"Look, there's the intercom." Kenny pointed to a little box at the side of the gate. "All we have to do is buzz the house, and then they'll open the gates."

"Don't be daft, Kenny!" Lyndz exclaimed. "They're not going to let you in, just like that!"

"Yeah, what are you going to say if they ask who you are?" I pointed out.

Kenny shrugged. "I'll think of something!"

"You wouldn't dare, Kenny!" Fliss wailed.

"Watch me!" Kenny marched over to the intercom and pressed the buzzer. We all shrieked "*Kenny!*" – but it was OK, because no-one answered.

"Rats! No-one's home." Kenny pulled a face and wandered off up the road a little way, trying to peer through gaps in the tall fence.

"We could wait here for the owner to come back," I suggested.

"The car windows are blacked out," Rosie reminded me. "So we won't be able to see if Brad's in the car or not."

"We could stand here holding a big sign," Kenny called over her shoulder. "BRAD MARTIN – IF YOU'RE IN THE CAR, PLEASE STOP!!!"

"And if it isn't Brad, we'll look like complete prats!" I grinned.

We all hung around, wondering what to do next. Fliss was shivering like mad, but I don't know if that was because she was cold or just plain scared.

"Hey, come and look at this!"

Kenny had gone round a bend in the road out of sight, and now she was rushing back towards us, waving her arms in the air.

"She's seen a ghost!" Fliss screamed.

"Don't be daft!" Kenny scoffed. "Come and see what I've found!"

Curiously we followed her round the corner, where Kenny pointed gleefully at quite a big hole in the Haunted House's fence. A section of fence panel had come loose and was leaning away from the rest, leaving a gap.

"Right, let's go!" Kenny said, and began to squeeze through the hole. Fliss gave a shriek, and Lyndz and Rosie didn't look too happy either.

"Kenny!" I hissed. "You can't do that – it's trespassing!"

"No, it's not," Kenny argued. "It's not like we're going to do any damage or steal anything."

"But Brad's not there anyway," Lyndz said. "No-one's in."

"We can look for *clues*," Kenny said in a determined voice.

"What, you mean like a surfboard lying around the living room?" I asked sarcastically.

Kenny snorted. "I reckon you lot are just too chicken!" She turned and grinned at us as she scrambled through the gap. "Come on, I *dare* you!"

I looked at the others. "Well, I guess it wouldn't hurt," I said. "After all, we know no-one's in."

Rosie nodded, but Lyndz still didn't look that keen and Fliss was as white as a sheet.

"What if someone comes back and catches us?" Lyndz asked nervously.

"We'll be really cool and calm and make something up!" Kenny shrugged. "Just leave all the talking to me!"

"Maybe Lyndz and I could stay here and be look-outs—" Fliss began. Then she stopped and clutched Lyndz's arm. "What was *that*?"

"Ow! Fliss, you're hurting me!" Lyndz complained.

"I heard a noise!" Fliss whispered, her eyes almost popping out of her head. "It sounded like a footstep!"

"There's no-one here!" Kenny said impatiently. "Now are you coming with me, or are the rest of the Sleepover Club a load of CHICKENS?"

"We're not chickens," I retorted as I climbed through the gap. "We're just a bit more sensible than you, that's all!"

"Sensible's boring," Kenny grinned as Rosie followed us into the overgrown garden. We were surrounded by trees and shrubs so thick, we could hardly see the house or the driveway. "Come on, Lyndz."

"I will, as soon as Fliss gives me my arm back!" Lyndz replied, trying to pull herself free.

"Don't leave me here on my own!" Fliss wailed.

"Well, come with us, then!" Kenny called impatiently as Lyndz climbed through to join us.

Reluctantly Fliss followed her, looking as if she was having all her teeth pulled out one by one. She was halfway through the gap when she froze.

"What was *that*?" she whispered.

I looked round sharply. I'd heard it too that time.

"It's probably just a squirrel or something—" Kenny began.

Well, if it was, it was the biggest squirrel in the world, because suddenly we heard footsteps coming quickly towards us. We all nearly *freaked*. Then suddenly a loud voice boomed out from nowhere.

"WHAT DO YOU GIRLS THINK YOU'RE DOING?"

CHAPTER FIVE

This time we *all* screamed – even Kenny. A really tall man was rushing through the undergrowth towards us, waving a trowel in his hand. To make it worse, he looked just like the butler Lurch from *The Addams Family*! He had a dead white face and exactly the same haircut and he looked about eight feet tall. He probably wasn't, but he was still scary!

"Eeek!" Fliss was stuck halfway through the gap. "Help!"

"Move it, Fliss!" Kenny yelled urgently, giving her a shove. Fliss tumbled back out on to the pavement and there was a loud, ripping sound – it could have been her knickers, or it could have been her new skirt. None of us cared though, we were too busy trying to get out of there!

Kenny was last through the gap, just as Lurch stormed up to the fence panting furiously. Lucky for us he wasn't very fit, or he might have caught us!

"This is private property!" he shouted furiously. "You're trespassing! Keep away from now on, or I'll call the police!"

We all ran for it. We legged it round the corner and along the road to Rosie's house. Fliss was nearly crying, and I didn't feel too brilliant myself.

"That was close!" Kenny breathed as we skidded to a halt outside the Cartwrights' gate.

"I thought you were going to be cool and calm," I reminded her bitterly. "Leave all the talking to you, you said!"

"Yeah, well, I didn't know we were going to come face to face with a Lurch look-alike!" Kenny retorted. "He must have been doing some gardening, and didn't hear us ring the buzzer."

"Ow! I've skinned both my knees getting through that stupid hole!" Rosie complained.

"And I've – hic – got the hiccups now!" Lyndz groaned. You know we call her the Hiccup Queen!

"I've ripped a hole in the back of my new skirt!" Fliss wailed. "My mum's going to kill me!"

"Not one of your better ideas, Kenny," I said, as Fliss almost stood on her head lifting up her coat and trying to see what she'd done to her skirt.

"Aha! But at least we know now that Brad *is* staying in the Haunted House!" Kenny said triumphantly.

We all stared at her as if she'd gone mad.

"How do you work *that* one out?" Rosie asked.

"You reckon Lurch was Brad in disguise, do you?" I asked, raising my eyebrows. "Well, he certainly had me fooled!"

"Don't be a smartypants, Francesca," Kenny shrugged. "It's obvious, isn't it? Lurch is Brad's bodyguard!"

We all considered that. It made sense.

After all, Lurch was enough to scare off anyone!

"You *could* be right, Kenny," I said slowly. "You're not as stupid as you look!"

"Nobody could be that stupid!" Fliss muttered. "Can you see my knickers?"

"No, it's a really small hole," I told her. "Your mum probably won't even notice."

"She'll notice," Fliss said gloomily.

"It's really annoying," Kenny grumbled as we gazed across the road at the Haunted House. "If only we knew for *sure* whether Brad was there…"

We all gazed longingly at the gates of the Haunted House. Was hunky Brad Martin really living there – or not?

"Look!" Fliss squealed in horror. "There's Lurch again!"

We all nearly jumped out of our skins. Sure enough, Lurch was standing by the gates peering up and down the road – looking for us, probably!

"Quick!" Rosie flung open the gate, and we charged into the Cartwrights' garden and ducked down behind the tall hedge out of sight.

"Has he – hic – gone yet?" Lyndz whispered after a few minutes.

"Has who gone?" said a voice behind us.

We all nearly died of shock! Rosie's mum had come out of the house and was standing there, staring at us.

"Er – no-one, Mum," Rosie muttered.

Mrs Cartwright frowned. "What are you doing hiding behind our hedge? I thought you were going to visit Mrs Andrews this afternoon."

"We are," Rosie said quickly, herding us out of the gate again.

"'Bye, Mrs Cartwright!" we all chorused brightly. Rosie's mum obviously thought we'd all gone completely mad!

Lyndz was looking pleased. "Hey, the shock of your mum creeping up on us like that cured my hiccups, Rosie!"

"We'll have to think of a plan to sort Lurch out," Kenny frowned. "Or we'll never get to meet Brad."

"There is *no way* I'm going near the Haunted House again," Fliss announced firmly as we walked through the village to

Mrs Andrews' place. "The rest of the Addams Family might be inside, for all we know!"

Anyway, when we got to Mrs Andrews' house, the old lady seemed dead pleased to see us. I couldn't help wondering if she got many visitors, but at least she had loads of Christmas cards on her mantelpiece, so that was something. She wanted to give us some orange squash and biscuits, so we went into the kitchen to give her a hand. It was a bit of a mess so we helped her tidy up and put things away. Kenny even did some washing-up – that's how much she liked Mrs A!

"So, girls, what did you get for Christmas?" Mrs Andrews asked us when we'd wolfed down all the biccies. The major stress of escaping from Lurch (twice!) had left us all starving! "Anything nice?"

Fliss opened her mouth, and Kenny groaned.

"Don't start, Fliss. We don't want to be here till *next* Christmas!"

Mrs Andrews chuckled. "You got a lot of presents, did you, Fliss? Things are a bit different now from when I was a kid. We were lucky to get a bag of sweets, a ball and an orange in our Christmas stockings!"

"An *orange*?" Fliss's eyes almost popped out of her head.

"Yes, it was traditional," Mrs Andrews explained with a twinkle in her eyes. "We always had an orange each, stuffed right in the toe of the sock!"

The rest of us grinned at Fliss's face. I could just imagine what she'd say if *she* found an orange in her Christmas stocking!

"One year I got a top and whip," Mrs Andrews went on. "I don't suppose you girls know what that is, but you had to spin the top, and then use the whip to keep it spinning as long as you could..."

While Mrs Andrews was talking, I just happened to glance out of the living room window. Lucky I did. Because it was right at that very moment that I saw BRAD MARTIN go past!

CHAPTER SIX

I almost fell off the sofa! I could only see the top half of him, but Brad was wearing a dark-coloured fleece and a baseball cap, just like Rosie and the Goblin had said!

"It's Brad!" I spluttered, nudging Kenny who was drinking her squash.

"Ow!" Kenny almost took a bite out of the glass as her teeth clattered against it. "What did you say, Frankie?"

"Nothing," I muttered. I wanted to jump up and rush out right away, but I didn't want to offend Mrs Andrews. If I said we were leaving to chase after an Australian soap star, she'd have thought we were bananas! She might even have thought it was just a pathetic excuse to get away.

"Actually, it's time we were going." I jumped to my feet, hoping Brad would still be somewhere around by the time we got outside. "My mum said I had to be back by four."

"Did she?" Rosie asked. "You never said."

"Why've you got to be back by four?" Kenny asked nosily, and I could have thumped her!

"I just *do*." I eyeballed Kenny, who shrugged and got up from the sofa.

"I haven't finished my squash yet," Fliss said, and I could have thumped her too!

"I *really* need to be home *soon*!" I said sternly. I had my back to Mrs Andrews so I started pulling gruesome faces at Fliss. She nearly choked on her drink.

"What's the matter with *you*, Frankie?"

"Come on, lazybones." Lyndz hauled Fliss to her feet. "We'll come and see you again soon, Mrs Andrews."

"Shall we help you wash up the glasses?"

Rosie asked politely, and I could have screamed!

Luckily Mrs A shook her head. "No, I'll do that. Off you go. I've really enjoyed seeing you again, girls."

I rounded everyone up like a sheepdog and hurried them over to the front door. With any luck, we might still be in time to catch Brad!

"How would you like to come to lunch sometime soon?" Mrs Andrews went on as she opened the door. "I don't often get the chance to cook a big meal these days."

"That'd be great!" Rosie said, and the others nodded. Meanwhile, I had one foot out of the door, and I was just itching to get away!

"How about Wednesday at twelve o'clock?" Mrs A suggested.

"OK, but we'll have to check with our parents first," Lyndz said.

"I don't know if I can come on Wednesday," Fliss remarked. "We might be going out."

"We'll ring up and let you know for sure," Kenny told Mrs A.

I was practically having a heart attack by this time! Finally we said our goodbyes, and I was first out of the door – but you've guessed it. There was absolutely no sign of Brad. I groaned and buried my head in my hands.

Meanwhile the others were staring at me like I'd gone crazy.

"What's up with you?" Kenny asked.

"I saw Brad Martin!" I wailed. "He went past Mrs Andrews' window!"

"NO!" the others all gasped together.

"YES!" I snapped. "Why do you think I was trying to get you all out so quickly?"

"Well, where's he gone?" Fliss was dancing up and down impatiently as if she had ants in her pants.

"He went thataway!" I pointed down the road.

We charged off in that direction, nearly knocking Mrs Andrews' gate off the hinges when we all tried to push through it at the same time.

But there was no sign of Brad when we got to the corner of the road. There were several other streets which he could have gone down, leading off this one, as well as the park which was a short cut to the other side of the village.

"He could be *anywhere*!" Fliss wailed.

"No, I know which way he's gone!" Kenny said triumphantly. "He's on his way back to the Haunted House!"

"Come on, we can take the short cut through the park!" I yelled. "Brad might not know about that!"

We were about to rush towards the park when guess who we saw coming up the road towards us? The Queen and the Goblin!

"Act normal!" Kenny hissed urgently. "We don't want them to guess we're chasing Brad!"

We slowed down as the M&Ms got closer. Emma Hughes had on this pink fake fur coat with a matching hat and gloves that she must have got for Christmas. She looked like a snooty pink elephant.

"Quick, ring the zoo!" Kenny shouted as the M&Ms got nearer. "One of their animals has escaped!"

"Take no notice, Emma," the Goblin snapped as they stomped past us, noses in the air. "They're just jealous— *eek!*"

We all sniggered as Emily Berryman stepped right in this massive puddle and splattered Emma with dirty water!

"You idiot, Emily!" Emma shouted, her face as pink as her coat. "Look what you've done!"

"Come on," Kenny said in a low voice. "Let's get out of here!"

We left the M&Ms arguing and hurried through the park gates. There was still no sign of Brad, but Kenny was right. He *had* to be making his way back to the Haunted House.

"Oh no!" Kenny groaned as at last we all pounded round the corner of Rosie's street, gasping for breath. "Look!"

The Haunted House's electric gates were closing, and we just caught a glimpse of a figure in a baseball cap disappearing up the drive.

"It's him!" I wheezed.

"Brad!" Fliss wailed. "Come back!"

"We're not giving up yet!" Kenny said in a determined voice, and she marched over to .

the intercom and pressed the buzzer. The next moment we heard Lurch's voice loud and clear, and Fliss nearly wet herself!

"Yes?"

"We're here to see Brad Martin," Kenny said boldly.

Lurch snorted. "There's no-one of that name here," he said snootily. He must have been taking lessons from Emma Hughes! "You've got the wrong house."

"Rats!" Kenny muttered as the intercom was switched off. "He *would* say that! Come on, I'll get in through the fence again!"

We all nearly *died*.

"Forget it, Kenny," I said firmly.

"Lurch'll eat you alive!" Lyndz said.

"And if he complains to my mum, she'll kill me!" Rosie said.

"I'm not going through that fence again!" Fliss snapped. "No way!"

"I didn't say *us*, I said *me*," Kenny said, heading off round the corner. "I'll go in and get Brad's autograph on my own if you lot are too chicken to come with me—"

She stopped. The gap in the fence had

now been firmly boarded up. The rest of us heaved a sigh of relief, but Kenny looked really annoyed.

"What now?" Rosie asked.

"OK, guys, we'll come here tomorrow and stake out the house!" Kenny said in a really awful American accent. "Then when Brad comes out, we'll grab him!"

"No way!" Fliss screeched. "What about Lurch? What if he comes along and sees us?"

"Aha!" Kenny grinned. "That's where my masterplan comes in! Listen up, guys…"

"I can't believe I'm actually doing this!" I grumbled as we left Rosie's house and crossed the road. "Kenny, will you stop bumping into me all the time!"

"Sorry, I can't see very well with these glasses on!" Kenny squinted at me from behind her mum's specs. They were miles too big for her, and with her baseball cap jammed on top of her head and all her hair tucked inside, she looked ridiculous!

Kenny's 'masterplan' was that we *disguise* ourselves so Lurch wouldn't recognise us when we staked out the Haunted House. In fact, if he saw us he'd probably call the police straight away because we looked like a bunch of weirdos. Fliss was wearing loads of make-up she'd borrowed from her mum, Lyndz had put blue streaks in her hair with hair mascara and Rosie and me were wearing sunglasses (yeah, in December!). We'd all borrowed clothes from various members of our families, so none of us were wearing things that fitted. We looked like total rejects!

"Kenny, will you stop stepping on the bottoms of my trousers!" Rosie grumbled as we peered through the gates. She'd borrowed a pair of Tiffany's combat pants and they were way too long.

"Sorry." Kenny moved away from her, blinking behind her glasses, and bumped into me for about the millionth time.

"My skirt keeps falling down," Fliss grumbled. She was wearing one of her mum's posh skirts and these high heels she could hardly walk in!

"I hope it doesn't rain," Lyndz said anxiously. "I don't think this blue stuff's waterproof."

"Oh, stop moaning, you lot!" Kenny ordered us sternly. "It'll all be worth it when we see Brad Martin coming down the drive towards us!"

"What about *Frankie's mum* coming down the street towards us?" Lyndz said, looking worried.

Sure enough, there was my mum walking along the other side of the road and pushing Izzy in her buggy!

"Oh, rats!" I hissed. "She must be going to see your mum, Rosie!"

"Mum never mentioned it!" Rosie wailed.

"Quick, turn round and pretend to look through the gates," Kenny hissed. "She won't know it's us."

We all turned round and stood with our backs to my mum.

"She'll never recognise us," Fliss said confidently. "Our disguises are too brilliant!"

"Hello, girls," we heard my mum call. "What are you up to?"

We all groaned and turned round again.

"Nothing, Mum," I called back.

My mum raised her eyebrows as she took in our ragbag appearance: mine and Rosie's sunglasses, Fliss's make-up, Lyndz's blue hair and Kenny's specs.

"Oh, really?" she said coolly, pushing Izzy across the road. "I didn't know you were going to a fancy-dress party today."

We were well and truly rumbled!

"OK, OK," I said crossly. Sometimes only the truth will do! "We think Brad Martin might be staying in the Haunted House, and we're waiting for him to come out."

"What are the disguises for?" my mum asked.

That floored us a bit – we didn't want to tell her that Lurch had caught us breaking and entering. But luckily just then Izzy took one look at Fliss's make-up, and started to bawl.

"Ssh, it's all right," my mum said, rocking the buggy until Izzy calmed down. "I don't know why you think Brad Martin's living here," she went on. "There's only Mr Pearce and his son Jonathan in the house as far as I know."

We all did a double-take.

"*What?*" I said.

"Our firm did the paperwork when Mr Pearce bought the house," my mum replied. "I think they keep themselves very much to themselves, although I've seen Jonathan out and about in the village sometimes."

"Does he wear a baseball cap?" I asked, my heart sinking.

"And a dark-coloured fleece?" Rosie added gloomily.

My mum nodded. "I think you've got your wires crossed, girls," she said. "And now you'd better go and get rid of those disguises before you frighten Izzy any more!"

"If only you'd asked your mum who was living in the house, Frankie!" Fliss moaned as we trailed after my mum towards Rosie's house.

"*Sor-ree!*" I retorted. "But I didn't think my mum knew anything about it."

"Lurch must be Mr Pearce," Kenny said in disgust. "And all those so-called sightings of Brad must have been Jonathan Pearce!"

"Well, he *does* look a *bit* like Brad," Rosie said defensively.

Kenny groaned. "I'm sick of the name Brad Martin!" she said. "And it wasn't even him!"

"As if Brad would be staying in Cuddington!" Fliss chimed in.

"We must've been mad to even think it!" Lyndz added.

"Right," I said, looking round at everyone. "So Brad Martin's not in Cuddington, and we're not going to spend any more time hunting him down. Agreed?"

"Agreed!" everyone said.

So that was that.

Or was it?

CHAPTER SEVEN

"So when are we having this Australian sleepover, then?" Kenny asked impatiently as we walked down the High Street towards the newsagents. We reckoned we deserved a whole load of sweeties to cheer us up, now that we definitely knew Brad wasn't in Cuddington.

"What about New Year's Eve?" Lyndz said hopefully. But Kenny was already shaking her head.

"Nah, my parents are having a big family party," she said.

"And we're going to my gran's," Fliss chimed in.

"What about the night we go to the panto?" Rosie suggested. "That'd be an excellent time to have the Australian sleepover, after we've seen Brad!"

"Yeah, but we won't have time to *do* anything," I pointed out as I pushed open the newsagent's door. "We won't get back from the panto till quite late."

The newsagent's was nearly empty, but guess who was in there? Our two most *favourite* people in the whole world – NOT! The Goblin was buying a copy of *Cool!* magazine, and the Queen was choosing a bag of crisps. They glanced up as we came in, and then they started grinning and nudging each other. For one horrible moment I thought that perhaps Brad *was* staying in Cuddington, and they'd sussed out where he was. But it wasn't that at all – although it was nearly as bad!

"Hey, Emma, I'm really looking forward to going to the panto on Saturday to see Brad," Emily Berryman said loudly. "Especially as we've got *front-row seats*!"

Eek! I glanced at the others. That meant

the M&Ms were going to the panto the same night as *we* were! We had quite good seats, but they weren't in the front row. It was completely sick-making! We all gritted our teeth and pretended not to be listening. But the Queen and the Goblin were really out to rub our noses in it this time.

"Ooh, I *know*," Emma agreed. "And don't forget we'll be going backstage to meet Brad too!"

This time we all nearly burst a bloodvessel! Going backstage? *Meeting Brad???*

"Isn't it *lucky* my dad's friend knows the theatre manager?" Emma went on smugly.

"Ooh, *very* lucky," the Goblin cooed. "So we'll get Brad's autograph whether he's staying in Cuddington or not!" And they both swanned out, looking like cats who'd swallowed a whole carton of cream!

"Right, let me at them!" Kenny rushed over to the door. "I'm going to shove the Queen's fake fur hat right down her throat!"

"Kenny, calm down!" I ordered, grabbing her arm. "They were just trying to wind us up."

"Well, it worked!" Rosie said dismally.

"They're going backstage and meeting Brad!" Fliss wailed. "Lucky things!"

"We'll never hear the end of it!" Kenny growled.

Lyndz was staring at a copy of the local newspaper on the shelves in front of us.

"Look at this," she said, but no-one took any notice.

"The M&Ms have really got one over on us this time," I said gloomily. "They'll have Brad's autograph, and we'll have zilch!"

"I bet they get their photo taken with Brad too," Rosie muttered.

"They'll be going on about it at school for *days*," Kenny groaned.

"I hate them!" Fliss sniffed.

"I'VE GOT SOMETHING TO SHOW YOU LOT IF YOU COULD JUST SHUT UP FOR ONE MINUTE!" Lyndz yelled.

We all nearly jumped out of our skins. That wasn't like Lyndz!

"Thank you," Lyndz said calmly as we all stared at her. (Meanwhile the shop assistant was glaring at the lot of us.) "Will you *please* have a look at this!"

She pointed to a paragraph at the bottom of the front page of the local newspaper.

Panto Star Makes Shopping Centre Appearance

Brad Martin, star of Australian soap opera *South Beach*, and also of *Aladdin,* this year's pantomime at the Unicorn Theatre, will be signing autographs in the Galleries shopping centre on Wednesday December 30th from three o'clock. Anyone wanting an autograph will be requested to make a small donation to local children's charities.

We all cheered and started doing high fives.

"This is our chance, guys!" Kenny exclaimed.

OK, maybe it wasn't as exciting as going backstage after the panto and meeting Brad.

And OK, there were going to be hundreds of other Brad fans in the shopping centre getting his autograph. But it was better than nothing.

"That's the day we're going to Mrs Andrews' for lunch," Lyndz pointed out. "But we should have plenty of time to do both."

"So all we've got to do now is persuade one of the oldies to take us," I said, looking round for volunteers.

"My parents won't," Kenny said. "They're too busy getting ready for the party."

"We've still got all our relatives staying with us," Lyndz remarked.

"My mum's got too much college work," Rosie said.

"And my mum's too pregnant," Fliss added.

I sighed as everyone looked hopefully at me. "Looks like it's *my* mum, then! Come on, we'd better go and ask her."

We immediately legged it out of the shop without buying anything, which meant the assistant behind the counter gave us a very dirty look.

"Let me do all the talking," I told everyone as we headed back to my place. "I know how to handle my mum."

"OK," everyone agreed.

Gran had taken Izzy to the park, and my mum was watching an old film on TV. She didn't look too pleased when we all trooped in.

"What have you lot been up to *now*?" she asked.

"Nothing, Mum," I said sweetly. "We just wanted to ask you something—"

"Oh, Mrs Thomas!" Fliss burst out pleadingly. "Will you *please* take us to see Brad Martin on Wednesday?"

"He's signing autographs in the Galleries shopping centre in Leicester," Rosie said breathlessly, "and none of the other oldies – I mean, parents – can take us!"

"Yeah, and the M&Ms have got front-row seats at the panto, *and* they're going backstage to meet Brad," Kenny explained. "And they're really going on about it!"

"We'd be *really* grateful, Mrs Thomas," Lyndz added.

So much for keeping quiet and letting me do the talking, I thought crossly. I just hoped they hadn't blown it!

"All right," said my mum.

I think we all nearly dropped down dead with shock, especially me!

"What?" I said.

"I said all right." My mum raised her eyebrows. "But on one condition..."

"What?" I asked again, expecting *behave yourselves, don't show me up, do as you're told, blah, blah, blah* – you know, parent-type things.

My mum grinned. "That you don't wear *any* of that stuff you were wearing this morning, OK?"

"Do you think I should wear the white top or the pink one?" Fliss asked with a frown. "Maybe I should change out of this skirt – I've gone off it."

Kenny groaned. "Oh, for goodness' sake, Fliss – make your mind up!"

"Not everyone lives in football shirts and trackie bottoms, Laura McKenzie!" Fliss retorted. "Help!" She dodged as Kenny chucked a pillow at her. "Mind my hair!"

It was Wednesday, the great day when we were *finally* going to meet Brad! We'd all met up round my house to get ready, then we were going to walk to Mrs Andrews for lunch and my mum was going to pick us up from there at two-thirty to drive into Leicester.

'Course, we were all pretty hyped up about it. We'd been fighting over the mirror for the last hour, doing our hair, putting on nail varnish and lip gloss and getting dressed up. Fliss had brought about a million different outfits with her and she couldn't decide which one to wear!

"It's time you were off to Mrs Andrews'," my mum called up the stairs. "Are you girls ready yet?"

"No, Fliss is standing here in her knickers!" Kenny called back.

Anyway, we managed to get Fliss to decide which skirt to put on, and we set off. Of course, we talked about Brad all the way there and what we were going to say when we came face to face with the man himself.

But when we got to Mrs Andrews' house, we got a bit of a shock that took our minds right off Brad.

For a start, the house looked empty. All the curtains were drawn, and the milk was still on the step outside.

"That's funny," I frowned. "It looks like there's no-one in."

"Ring the doorbell, Lyndz," Kenny said.

We waited for what seemed like ages, but nobody came, not even when Lyndz rang the bell a second time. Then Kenny lifted up the letterbox and yelled "Mrs Andrews! It's us!" really loudly, but still nothing.

"There's definitely no-one in," Lyndz said. "She would have heard that!"

"Maybe she forgot," Fliss suggested. "Old people do forget things sometimes."

"Shall we go back to Frankie's place, then?" Rosie asked.

Kenny was looking worried. "We ought to make sure Mrs Andrews is OK," she said. "Lots of my dad's elderly patients have had accidents around the home. What if she's hurt, and she can't get to the door?"

"What shall we do?" I asked.

Kenny nodded at the padlocked side gate which led into the back garden. "Let's climb over that and have a look round the back of the house," she suggested. "It's not very high."

"Not very high?" Fliss squeaked. "How am I supposed to get over that in my mini-skirt?"

"Don't be such a feeble girly, Fliss!" Kenny said sternly, hauling herself up on to the top of the gate. "Come on, give me your hand and Frankie'll give you a bunk-up."

"Yeah, go on, Fliss." Lyndz gave her a nudge. "Mrs Andrews might be in trouble."

Fliss didn't moan any more, but she was a bit pale as, between us, Kenny and I hoisted her up on top of the gate.

"Now just drop down the other side," Kenny instructed her.

"Aargh!"

We heard a loud thud as Fliss hit the ground.

"Are you OK, Fliss?" I called, trying not to laugh.

"Yeah," Fliss called weakly. "At least I didn't rip my skirt this time!"

The rest of us got over the gate, no bother, and then we hurried round to the back of the house.

Kenny stuck her nose right up against the kitchen window and peered in. Then she gave a gasp.

"Look!"

We all pressed our faces to the glass and stared inside. Poor old Mrs Andrews was lying on the kitchen floor in a heap, her eyes closed. For one horrible minute I thought she might be dead or something, but then Kenny rapped on the glass, and she opened her eyes and saw us.

"She's trying to say something!" Rosie said urgently. "What is it?"

"I think she's saying there's a spare key somewhere," Kenny muttered.

"Where?" I asked, straining my ears to hear. Mrs Andrews must have been pretty weak because she could hardly raise her voice above a whisper.

"Under the brick by the back door!" Lyndz cried, and we all dashed over there. Sure enough, there was a brick lying by a pot of flowers, and a key underneath it. Quickly I unlocked the door and we all rushed in.

"Oh, thank goodness you've come, girls!" Mrs Andrews said shakily. "I slipped and fell, and I think I've broken my leg. I heard you yelling through my letterbox and I tried to call for help, but I just couldn't shout loud enough."

"Don't worry, just lie still," Kenny told her. "I'm going to call an ambulance right away, and I'll call my dad too." And she rushed into the hall and grabbed the phone.

CHAPTER EIGHT

"Well done, girls!" Dr McKenzie said as the paramedics carried Mrs Andrews out of the house on a stretcher. "I'm really proud of you."

We all turned a bit red and stared down at our feet. We weren't used to hearing the oldies say things like that. We were more used to getting yelled at and told off!

"Is Mrs Andrews going to be OK?" Fliss asked anxiously as the ambulance drove off.

"Well, the paramedics think she might have a broken leg," Dr Mackenzie replied, "but we'll have to wait and see." He glanced at his watch. "I'll drop you all off at Frankie's house, and then I'll go to the hospital. I know Mrs Andrews hasn't got many relatives in this part of the world, so I'll just make sure she's OK."

"Hasn't she got *anyone* who can come and visit her?" Lyndz asked.

"Well, she has a sister up in Scotland." Dr McKenzie opened the car doors and motioned to us to get in. "But she's even older then Mrs Andrews, and it's a long way to travel. Apart from that, all her family is overseas, I think."

I thought that sounded a bit miserable, and so did the others by the looks on their faces.

"Can we come to the hospital with you, Dad?" Kenny asked suddenly, and the rest of us nodded.

"Are you sure?" Dr McKenzie raised his eyebrows. "We could be in for a long wait, and aren't you supposed to be going to see Bob Martin or someone?"

"*Brad* Martin," I said, trying not too feel too disappointed. "Oh, we can see him at the panto."

"We'd rather go to the hospital," Fliss said bravely.

"Mrs Andrews ought to have *some* visitors," Rosie added.

"Yeah," Lyndz agreed. "Anyway, we want to know if she's OK."

Dr McKenzie shrugged and started the engine. "Well, all right, if that's what you want."

We all sat in silence as we drove to the hospital. I guess we were all pretty down in the dumps about missing Brad, but what else could we do? We couldn't leave Mrs Andrews on her own.

When we got to the hospital, Dr McKenzie phoned our parents to tell them what was going on, and to tell my mum not to bother picking us up from Mrs Andrews' house. My mum said that if there was still time, she'd come and pick us up from the hospital and we could go to Leicester from there, but you know what hospitals are like. We waited and waited and waited... Even Dr McKenzie trying to pull a few strings didn't make any difference.

Finally, at about half past four, a doctor came over to speak to Kenny's dad. By this time we were just about climbing the waiting-room walls with boredom.

"What did he say, Dad?" Kenny demanded when the doctor had gone.

"Mrs Andrews has a broken leg and cuts and bruises, but apart from that, she's fine," Dr McKenzie replied.

"Can we see her?" I asked eagerly.

Dr McKenzie nodded. "But only for two minutes," he said firmly. "She's been through quite an ordeal, and she needs to rest."

Mrs Andrews was in a room on her own just down the corridor. Her leg was done up in plaster and was held up off the bed by one of those pulley things, and she was lying with her eyes closed when we all tiptoed in. I thought she might be asleep, but at last she opened her eyes.

"Have you been here all this time, girls?" she asked weakly.

"Sure we have!" Kenny said. "We wanted to make sure you were OK."

"Thanks to you, I will be," Mrs A said. "You

know what, Dr McKenzie, if it hadn't been for these girls, I might still be lying there in my kitchen right now…"

Her voice drifted away and her eyes shut again. Kenny's dad opened the door, and we all filed out.

"Well, girls," he said as we went towards the exit, "I never thought I'd say this, but you're heroines!"

"*Are* we?" Fliss looked thrilled.

"Yeah, you're definitely a heroine, Fliss!" Kenny said wickedly. "It was pretty heroic of you getting over the gate in *that* mini-skirt!"

OK, so maybe we hadn't managed to see Brad Martin and get his autograph, but it was still a pretty nice feeling to know that we'd helped someone and that we were *heroines*!

And we had an even bigger shock in store. We all went back to Kenny's house, and the car had hardly pulled up outside when the front door opened and all these parents came pouring out! There was my mum, dad and Izzy, Fliss's mum, Mrs Cartwright and Mr and Mrs Collins with Lyndz's little brothers

Ben and Sam. It was like a Sleepover Club Parents' meeting!

"What are you all doing here?" I gasped as everyone started hugging us.

"Well, we had to come and congratulate our heroines, didn't we?" my dad said, ruffling up my hair which I usually hate – but funnily enough, today I didn't mind.

"Yes, well done, girls." Mrs Collins gave Lyndz a hug. "How's Mrs Andrews?"

"She's got a broken leg, but she'll be fine," Dr McKenzie replied. "Thanks to this lot!"

"It was a shame you had to miss seeing Brad Martin," my mum said consolingly, "but you did the right thing, girls."

We all looked glum when my mum said that. We were glad we'd helped Mrs Andrews, but now we'd have to listen to the M&Ms crowing about meeting Brad Martin for ever after! Going back to school after the holidays would be a nightmare.

"Actually, girls, we were thinking..." Kenny's mum smiled at us. "If you promise not to get under my feet tonight while I'm getting ready for our New Year's Eve party, maybe..."

"Maybe we can have a sleepover?" Kenny broke in, her face splitting into a big grin. "Our *Australian* sleepover! Can we, Mum? Really?"

"Well, we think you deserve it!" Mrs McKenzie said, and we all cheered madly.

"Right, we've got to talk in Australian accents for the whole sleepover!" Kenny ordered us as she pranced around the living room in her shorts and T-shirt and her hat with corks hanging off it. (It was really a sombrero that Kenny's gran had brought back from Spain, but it looked OK.) We were all wearing shorts and T-shirts too. It was lucky the McKenzies had their central heating going full blast, or we would have been freezing. "G'day, mates, how y'doing?"

"That sounds Irish!" Fliss objected. "Anyway, I can't talk Australian."

"I can, mate – no worries," Lyndz said, but she wasn't much better than Kenny!

"That sounds sort of *Russian*!" I grinned.

"OK, forget the Aussie accents." Kenny

rolled her eyes. "I wonder how the barbie's coming on?"

"I feel really sorry for your dad out there in the cold," Rosie said as we looked out into the garden. Dr McKenzie was all wrapped up in a big overcoat, getting the barbie going! I mean, you can't have an Australian sleepover without a barbie, can you?

Meanwhile, Kenny's mum was in the kitchen cooking stuff for their New Year's Eve party, and Kenny's sisters were both out. Molly the Monster was totally disgusted that we'd become heroines, so Kenny was well chuffed.

"Quick, *South Beach* is about to start!" Fliss yelled, and we all raced over to the sofa. This would be the very first episode since before Christmas, and we were all really looking forward to it – we were getting serious Brad Martin withdrawal symptoms.

"OK – I now declare this Australian sleepover officially open!" Kenny announced just as the theme tune started. "Come on, you've got to sing it in an Australian accent! *Life is so hard, When you don't have that special someone…*"

But the rest of us couldn't sing at all – we were too busy rolling around on the sofa, killing ourselves laughing at Kenny's gruesome singing. Trying to sing with an Australian accent made her sound even *more* like a cat with a sore throat!

Anyway, it was *great* seeing Brad again after all this time. He managed to get up out of his hospital bed and go surfing, *and* he overpowered the escaped convict who was holding Andrew and Noelene hostage, so he was the hero of the whole episode. Not bad for someone who'd been ill for the last few weeks. Oh, and he finally decided he wanted to go out with Charlene, not Melanie, so Kenny was well pleased!

"Grub's up!" Dr McKenzie called just as *South Beach* finished. "Hurry up before it gets as cold as I am!"

We wrapped ourselves up and charged outside. We were *starving*. Kenny's dad had cooked loads of burgers and sausages (and veggie ones for me), and we wolfed the whole lot down in about five minutes. By the time we'd finished, there wasn't a bite of burger or a scrap of sausage left on the barbie. Kenny had even made wichity grubs out of marzipan for pud, although I didn't see Fliss have any.

"I'm c-c-c-cold!" Fliss started to moan eventually. Her nose did look a bit blue. So we all went back inside again, leaving poor old Dr McKenzie to clear up. He looked a bit blue himself when he finally came in and disappeared into his study.

"What shall we do now?" Rosie asked.

"I've got a quiz for you!" Kenny said gleefully, diving behind the sofa and pulling out this bulging sports bag.

"What kind of quiz?" Lyndz wanted to know.

"Famous Australians!" Kenny replied, taking her sombrero off and opening the bag. "But you'll have to give me a few minutes to get ready."

"OK." I grinned at the others. Knowing Kenny, this was bound to be good!

Kenny stood with her back to us for a few minutes, getting ready. When she turned round, she had glasses on and this grey curly wig – goodness knows where she'd got it from!

"Now look at this poor little dog," she began in a *terrible* Aussie accent. "The vet's going to take a look at his bad paw—"

"Rolf Harris – *Animal Hospital*!" I yelled.

"Correct!" Kenny said, whipping off the glasses. "Now what about this one?"

She put her sombrero on again, and then pulled this cuddly toy out of her bag. It was a little blue dolphin.

"Urgh! Argh!" Kenny rolled around on the carpet, pretending the dolphin was attacking her and trying to bite her neck. It was the funniest thing I've ever seen!

"Crocodile Dundee!" Rosie shouted as the rest of us fell about. "Kenny, that's not even a crocodile!"

"Well, it's not far off!" Kenny retorted.

"Girls, could one of you get that, please?" Mrs McKenzie called from the kitchen as the doorbell rang.

"I'll go." I jumped up from the sofa and ran down the hall. I didn't want to miss Kenny's next Famous Australian – they'd been the business so far!

Quickly I opened the McKenzies' front door. There was a guy in a baseball cap there – and I nearly fainted right on the spot.

Brad Martin was standing on the doorstep, smiling at me.

CHAPTER NINE

My mum says I'm never lost for words, but I was this time. I couldn't say *anything*. I just stood there with my mouth wide open, catching flies!

"Oh, hi," Brad said in this Australian voice, sounding just like he did on the telly. "Can I speak to Dr McKenzie please?"

I just stared at him. He was even better-looking in real life! His hair was blonder and his eyes were bluer, although he didn't look quite as tall as he did on the TV.

"Er – does Dr McKenzie live here?" Brad was starting to look worried. "Have I come to the right place?"

I just about managed to get my head together and answer him this time! "Er – yes, come in. The study's in the McKenzie over there – I mean, Dr McKenzie's in the study over there." I pointed across the hall, then I backed away towards the living room, still staring at Brad.

"Thanks," Brad said, giving me this *smile*! He knocked on the study door, and I turned and dashed into the living room, whooping my head off like someone on an American chat show!

"It's Brad!"

Kenny and the others all turned to stare at me.

"It's Brad!" I yelled, dancing up and down in front of them. "He's here!"

"Oh, sit down and shut up!" Kenny said impatiently. "I want to do my next Famous Australian."

"Brad Martin's *here*!" I shouted. "He's in the study with your dad!"

Kenny burst out laughing. "Nice try, Frankie!" She turned to the others. "I've just got one more thing to get," she said, and went out of the room.

"You don't understand!" I groaned. "Brad Martin's here – he's really here!"

"Shall we sit on her?" Rosie asked Fliss and Lyndz. They nodded and jumped on top of me!

"Nice one!" Kenny said approvingly as she came back in, carrying an ironing board. "That'll teach her to wind us up!"

"I'm not winding you up!" I spluttered, trying to push Rosie, Fliss and Lyndz off, and failing miserably. "Honestly!"

"OK, who am I *now*?" Kenny had put a mop on her head, and was posing with the ironing board.

"BRAD MARTIN!" Lyndz, Fliss and Rosie yelled together. I had no breath left to say anything because I was still getting crushed to bits!

"Did someone say my name?"

And Brad walked into the room, followed by Dr McKenzie.

Kenny, Rosie, Lyndz and Fliss all did exactly what I'd done. They froze completely, and didn't say a word!

"*Now* will you get off me!" I panted, struggling to get free. "I *told* you I wasn't winding you up!"

"Do you get this reaction wherever you go, Brad?" Dr McKenzie asked with a twinkle in his eyes. Fliss, Lyndz and Rosie looked as if they were in a trance, and I think it was only hanging on to the ironing board that was keeping Kenny from collapsing. Even Mrs McKenzie came in from the kitchen to see what was going on.

"Sometimes!" Brad said, looking embarrassed.

"But what are you *doing* here?" I asked. I was about the only Sleepover who could speak at the moment.

"I wanted to thank you girls for helping my aunt today," Brad said with a smile.

We were all so dazed, none of us had a *clue* what he meant! Luckily Dr McKenzie came to the rescue.

"Mrs Andrews is Brad's aunt – well, his great-aunt actually." He glanced at Brad, who nodded.

"Mrs Andrews?" we all said together, completely stunned.

"Yeah, I've been visiting her while I'm working in the panto," Brad explained. "I'm staying in a hotel in Leicester, but I get over to Cuddington whenever I can."

I glanced at the others. So Brad *had* been in Cuddington some of the time. Some of those sightings must have been real ones, and some of them must have been that guy from the Haunted House! No wonder we'd got into such a muddle!

"Mrs Andrews never *said*." Kenny was staring at Brad as if she suddenly expected him to disappear in a puff of smoke. I knew what she was thinking too – if we'd told Mrs Andrews we were looking for Brad, maybe we'd have got to meet him a whole lot sooner!

Brad looked embarrassed again. "Well, I suggested that she didn't tell anybody. I didn't want her getting bothered by fans or by the press." He grinned at us, and Fliss nearly melted into a little pool on the floor. I don't think the rest of us were far off either!

"Anyway, I just wanted to thank you for what you did today."

"Oh, that's all right," we chorused.

"I'm hoping to persuade my aunt to move to Australia to be with the rest of the family," Brad went on. "Dr McKenzie thinks it's a good idea."

"Um – Brad," Fliss squeaked, just about finding her voice after all this time. "Do you think we could have your autograph?"

"No worries!" Brad grinned. "I've got some publicity photos for the panto with me – I'll sign those for you."

So we all stood there while Brad signed these pics of himself looking really hunky in his Aladdin costume! He even asked us our names and wrote a *personal* message to each one of us. Mine said:

Thanks for all your help, Frankie love Brad Martin

Isn't that *cool*!

"Dr McKenzie tells me you're coming to the panto soon," Brad said as he finished signing Fliss's photo. I couldn't see what he'd written, but Fliss was practically fainting with delight.

"Yes, on Saturday," Rosie said shyly.

"Well, I'd like you to come as my guests," Brad went on, as we all looked at each other in delight. "Get your parents to return the tickets to the box office for a refund, and we'll see if we can fix you up with a box for the night if we've still got one free..."

This was just unbelievable!

"A box?" Fliss gasped. "I've never been in one of those before!"

"We'll be like the Royal Family!" Lyndz said, her eyes round.

"No probs, I'll sort that out, then," Brad said as he shook hands with Kenny's parents. Dr McKenzie ushered him over to the door. "See you again soon, girls!"

And then he was gone.

"Don't wash your hand, Mum!" Kenny ordered her as we all rushed over to the window just in time to see Brad climb into this really funky red sports car. "Brad Martin's touched that hand!"

"He seemed quite nice, didn't he?" Mrs McKenzie remarked, going back to the kitchen.

"He was gorgeous!" Fliss said dreamily.

"Much cuter than he is on the telly!" Rosie added.

"His eyes looked bluer," I said.

"And his hair looked blonder," Lyndz agreed.

"And we're going to be his special guests at the panto and we're going to sit in a box and look down on the M&Ms in their crummy front-row seats!" Kenny said gleefully. "I can't *wait*!"

CHAPTER TEN

"This is *class*!" Kenny grinned as we climbed the stairs to our box. It was the night of the panto, and we'd all got dressed up to the nines, including my mum and dad (Gran was babysitting Izzy). Even Kenny had left her Leicester City shirt at home for once, and was wearing a new white top.

As soon as we'd got to the theatre, an usherette had come over to us.

"Are you Brad Martin's special guests?" she asked, and all these people turned round and stared at us. Oh, it was so cool! The usherette led us up the stairs and showed us into our box, and it was *fab*. We had really comfy red velvet chairs with *cushions*! And there were boxes of sweets lying around as well as theatre programmes.

"If you want anything, just ring that buzzer over there," the usherette smiled as she left.

"This is the business!" I beamed, grabbing a box of liquorice allsorts.

"We've got a great view from here," Lyndz said excitedly, looking down at the stage.

"Isn't it nice of Brad to give us these sweets?" Fliss said, her mouth full of butterscotch.

"Look at everyone else in their boring old ordinary seats!" Rosie said, gazing down at the rest of the theatre where people were milling about underneath us.

"Yeah, we can drop sweets on their heads if we want to!" Kenny said gleefully.

"But we *don't* want to," my mum said in a warning voice.

"Yes, let's try and behave with a little class, shall we, Kenny?" my dad suggested with a grin. "After all, we *are* sitting in a box!"

"Yeah, I'd better practise waving at people,

then!" Kenny started waving like the Queen does, which made us all roar – especially when people started looking up at us. And guess who arrived just then?

"Look, it's the M&Ms!" Rosie hissed

The M&Ms, who were with Emma's mum, didn't notice us at first because they were too busy finding their seats. But then the Goblin happened to glance up, so we all started doing these queen-like waves. Emily nearly broke her neck looking up at us, and nudging the Queen at the same time. We all nearly died laughing at the look on their faces!

"Oh, that was just the best!" Kenny groaned, holding her sides.

"Serves them right for boasting about their front-row seats!" I said.

"Ssh!" Lyndz hissed as the lights began to dim. "It's starting!" And we all settled back in our comfy chairs with boxes of sweets on our laps.

The panto was *ace*. I bet you've been to loads of pantos? Well, think of the best one you've ever been to and this one was a hundred times better! I just wish you could have come to see it with us, but I'll try to tell you the best bits. The best bit was Brad as Aladdin (of course!), but everyone else wasn't bad either. The Princess was played by this children's TV presenter called Anthea Little and she had some gorgeous costumes, and Aladdin's friends Yin and Yang were played by two acrobats who kept flinging themselves around the stage and doing these fantastic stunts. One of the most amazing things was the genie of the lamp, who was a massive *hologram*! And best of all, we had a fantastic view from the box with no-one else's heads in the way!

The interval came round so fast, we were a bit disappointed – we were having such a great time, we didn't want it to end. But we soon cheered up when the usherette came into the box with ice-creams and drinks for everyone.

"You girls will have to be heroines more often!" my dad remarked as he handed the ice-creams round. "This is the best night out I've had for ages!"

Things got even better in the second half. Aladdin and his mates Yin and Yang were having one of those sing-songs that they always do in pantos – you know, when they divide the audience in half and see which half can sing the loudest? Well, Aladdin said they wanted some volunteers to go up on the stage and help him out.

"Rats!" Kenny whispered in my ear. "It's a shame we're stuck up here!"

"Look at Emma Hughes!" Fliss moaned. "She's jumped out of her seat as if there's a rocket up her bottom!"

Sure enough, Emma Hughes and Emily Berryman were scrambling to get out of their seats and be first up on to the stage.

"Wait a minute, folks!" Aladdin came to the front of the stage and shaded his eyes as he looked up at our box. "I think I can see some of my mates up there – Frankie, Fliss, Kenny, Lyndz and Rosie, will you come down and give me a hand?"

"YES!" we yelled, and we all rushed over to the door, nearly knocking my mum and dad off their chairs. We didn't have a clue how to get down to the stage, but the usherette was waiting on the stairs for us and she showed us the way. About two minutes later we were all on the stage with Brad, blinking under the bright lights.

"OK, here's the song we're going to sing," Brad announced, and a screen appeared with the words of the *South Beach* theme tune on it.

"Oh, great!" Kenny said, "we know this!" And everyone in the theatre laughed, except for the M&Ms, who were slumped back in their seats looking as if they were going to explode with fury. They just didn't have a clue *how* Brad knew our names, and it was driving them crazy!

Brad – I mean, Aladdin! – divided the audience into two sections. Yin and Yang had one side, and us and Brad had the other. The M&Ms were on Yin and Yang's side, and they were so determined not to let us win that they were really SCREECHING *"Life is so hard, When you don't have that special someone"* when it was their side's turn to sing, to try and make sure we didn't win. It was s-o-o pathetic! And it didn't work anyway – our side was the loudest.

"Thanks a lot, girls!" Brad said before we went back to our seats, and he gave us a *massive* box of chocs each while the audience applauded. We couldn't help grinning smugly at the M&Ms down in the front row!

But even *that* wasn't the best bit of the evening. The last part of the panto was the big scene where Aladdin marries the Princess, and everyone comes on to take a bow. We were cheering and clapping like mad when the usherette came into the box again.

"Brad would like you to meet him backstage," she said, and we all nearly *fainted*.

"Oh, please, please, *please* let the M&Ms be there, and see us talking to Brad!" Fliss prayed as we followed the usherette down the stairs again.

"I think we've rubbed their noses in it enough for one night, haven't we?" Lyndz grinned.

"NO!" the rest of us said together.

It was weird going backstage. People were running about packing props and costumes away, but Brad was waiting for us, still dressed up in his Aladdin clothes.

"Hello, girls," he said. "Hi, Mr and Mrs Thomas. We've got a reporter and photographer here from the local paper. They want to interview the girls about what happened with my aunt, and take a few pictures of us together. Is that OK with you?"

Was that OK with us! We were so thrilled, none of us could say a word!

"Well, I don't know—" my dad began.

"*Dad!*" I groaned.

My dad winked. "Just kidding! Of course it's all right."

So when the M&Ms came backstage clutching their autograph books, there we were, standing with Brad having our picture taken by the newspaper photographer, and being interviewed by the reporter!

"Say *cheese*!" the photographer called, but we didn't need to do that. All we had to do was look at the Queen and the Goblin's faces, and that made us smile the biggest smiles ever.

* * *

"I think that was the best night of my whole life!" Rosie sighed, eating her fourteenth chocolate.

"Me too," Lyndz agreed.

"I wish I had a photo of the M&Ms' faces when they came backstage," Kenny chortled.

"I can't wait to see our picture in the newspaper," I said.

"My favourite bit was when we sang the *South Beach* song on stage with *Brad*!" Fliss said dreamily.

Everyone was staying the night round at my place, and although it wasn't officially a sleepover, we'd decided to have a midnight feast. We were far too excited to go to sleep – I didn't think I'd ever get to sleep again! So we were all lying in a row on my bed in our pyjamas, scoffing the chocs Brad had given us.

"It's funny being heroines and not being in trouble, isn't it?" Kenny said lazily.

I leaned over and nicked a caramel cream from Rosie's box. "Let's enjoy it while it lasts!" I said, and we all cheered.

A moment later the door opened, and my mum came in, looking harassed.

"Sorry, Mrs Thomas, did we wake Izzy up?" Lyndz asked.

"It's not that," my mum replied. "Fliss, your Auntie Paula's coming to collect you straight away. Your mum's gone into hospital – the babies are coming!"

"Oh!" Panicking, Fliss jumped up and tried to walk across the bed over the rest of us. Chocolates flew everywhere as she knocked two of the boxes over.

"Yikes!" Kenny yelled as Fliss tripped over her leg.

"Ouch!" I winced as Fliss accidentally kicked my shin.

"Ow!" Rosie and Lyndz tried to dive out of Fliss's way and banged their heads together.

"Help!" Fliss got her foot caught in the duvet and ended up on the floor in a tangled heap. Meanwhile, Izzy had woken up and started to bawl!

"Looks like everything's back to normal, then," my mum remarked as she hurried out.

Sorry, we've got to go and help Fliss get changed and pack her sleepover bag now. You'll just have to wait till next time to hear about the new babies!

See ya!